KIRK SCROGGS

SNOOP TROOP

IT CAME FROM BENEATH THE PLAYGROUND

Little, Brown and Company
New York   Boston

Copyright © 2014 by Kirk Scroggs

Little, Brown and Company

Hachette Book Group
237 Park Avenue, New York, NY 10017
Visit our website at lb-kids.com

Little, Brown and Company is a division of Hachette Book Group, Inc.
The Little, Brown name and logo are trademarks of Hachette Book Group, Inc.

The publisher is not responsible for websites (or their content)
that are not owned by the publisher.

First Edition: September 2014

Library of Congress Cataloging-in-Publication Data

Scroggs, Kirk.
It came from beneath the playground / Kirk Scroggs.—First edition.
pages cm.—(Snoop troop ; 1)
Summary: "Fifth-grade private eyes Logan and Gustavo use their doodling and detective skills to solve the mystery of a group of moles that have stolen the amusement park merry-go-round."—Provided by publisher.
ISBN 978-0-316-24271-4 (paper over board)—ISBN 978-0-316-24273-8 (ebook)—ISBN 978-0-316-36453-9 (library edition ebook) [1. Mystery and detective stories. 2. Stealing—Fiction. 3. Moles (Animals)—Fiction. 4. Humorous stories.] I. Title.
PZ7.S436726It 2014
[Fic]—dc23
2013041706

10 9 8 7 6 5 4 3 2 1

RRD-C

Printed in the United States of America

To Isaac

*Special thanks to
Steve Deline; Joanna Stampfel-Volpe;
Diane, Corey, Candace, and Charlotte Scroggs;
Camilla and Marisa Deline; Joe Kocian;
Mark Mayes; and a twenty-one-Snoop-Troop
salute to Andrea Spooner, Deirdre Jones,
Tracy Shaw, and the whole Little, Brown crew.
Woo-hoo!*

An Important Message from the Narrator

Yo! Attention, all you wannabe detectives out there!

Justice needs your help. Some lowlife, sneaker-sniffin' criminal is stealing all the fun from the kids of Murkee Elementary School. Help my detectives put this creep behind bars. Examine each page of this case file closely for clues, especially if you see a magnifying glass like the one below. I'd help out, but I'm too busy looking for Rocco the Racketeering Raccoon. Now, where could that little fleabag be?

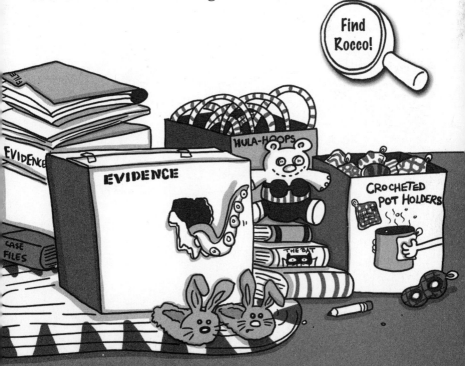

Find Rocco!

EVIDENCE

CASE FILES

EVIDENCE

HULA-HOOPS

THE BAT

CROCHETED POT HOLDERS

CHAPTER 1

BY THE BOOK

After school at Murkee Elementary...

Silence creeps over the halls like a spilled Blue Raspberry Icee....

Chalk dust settles on the cold classroom floors like volcanic ash....

Tumbleweeds roll through the empty playground, tumbling over and over, like a narrator who just won't shut up....

The day is Wednesday.
The time is 4:25 PM.
Remember that!
All that we hold dear
could depend on it!

That's fourth-grader Logan Lang sitting in the dark, dank library, just like she does every day after school, surrounded by her friends....

And when I say "friends," I mean mystery books,

crime novels,

and twisted tales of suspense....

They're all she has in this cold, lonely world.

Okay, I think they get it. I'm a little *too* into mystery books.

A BRIEF HISTORY OF LOGAN

This is her idea of being less nerdy.

Miss Perusa, the librarian, gives Logan just five more minutes to grab as many small, furry animal mystery books as she can find.

But before Logan can check out her giant stack of books, a voice blares out across the library!

ATTENTION, ALL UNITS!

It's coming from her combination police radio/ lunch box....

I REPEAT, ATTENTION, ALL UNITS!

It picks up a hundred frequencies and smells like bologna and corn chips.

Logan tries to gingerly tiptoe down the hall toward the exit when...

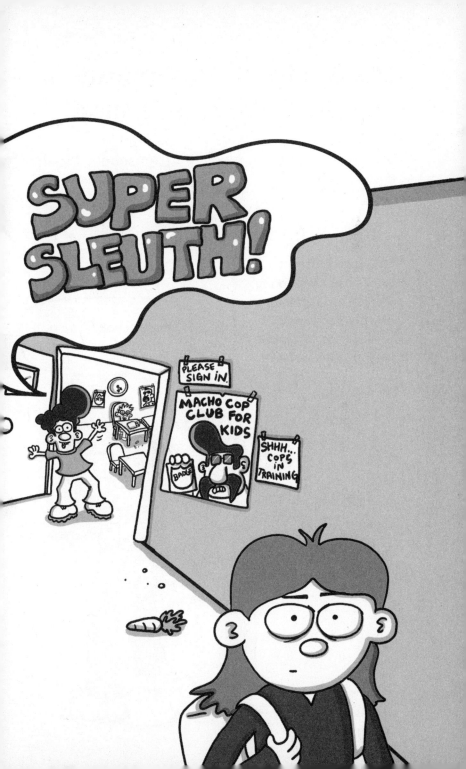

It's Gustavo Muchomacho, Logan's arch-nuisance!

He's conducting his weekly after-school Macho Cop Club for Kids meeting.

AN EVEN BRIEFER HISTORY OF GUSTAVO

AGE: 1 YEAR

AGE: 10 YEARS

17

CHAPTER 2
MERRY-GONE-MISSING

Hurling Rivers Amusement Park...

When Logan arrives, the place is taped off like an unopened birthday present and crawling with cops.

That's Captain Mosely of the Murkee City Police Department....

Sure enough, there's just a big hole in the ground where the carousel used to be.

I don't think you're supposed to go past that police tape.

Good point. Carry on.

What have you got there?

I didn't know you could draw.

That was nice of you.

While the cops eat the evidence, Logan sets out in search of her own clues. Somewhere on the deserted boardwalk, she gets the creepy sensation that someone is hiding nearby.

FROG LEAP

HOO

THE CLAW!

Suddenly,
a sniffly old man bursts out
of a pile of stuffed animals!

It's Izzy Hurling, owner of Hurling Rivers Amusement Park, and he's quite sneezy.

29

Listen to Old Man Hurling's description and draw the culprit on a piece of scratch paper, the chalkboard, or your mom's favorite tablecloth!

32

33

All of a sudden, a pint-size detective with two tons of attitude and a one-ton mustache is on the scene....

> Step aside, Officers! Detective Chuck Brawn is here to solve this carnival conundrum!

Something about this guy looks familiar. Logan can't quite place him, but she already has the urge to smack him with an overcooked bratwurst.

35

36

It's not Officer Chuck Brawn at all! It's Gustavo Muchomacho in a cheap fake mustache!

39

Ahem! Hey, you two, maybe you should team up like Captain Mosely suggested. Logan, with your smarts and Gustavo's...uh...enthusiasm, you could cause twice as much damage.

Well, how about it? Team Logan and Gustavo.

As Gustavo takes off, Logan is left all alone....

Guess we'll just have to see who solves the case first, the cops or me. *Adiós, muchacha!*

Before she heads home, a chill nips at her neck and a strange feeling comes over her—like an evil presence is still lurking close by.

PARK

HOT ROASTED SNOW CONES

Find the evil presence!

45

CHAPTER 3
THAT SINKING FEELING

The next morning, Logan arrives at school tired and cranky from staying up all night watching the news reports about the theft. The smell of trouble hangs like bad air freshener in a gas station bathroom. Everywhere she looks, she thinks she sees moles. Principal Shrub tries to keep nervous students calm.

Inside, the school is abuzz with stories of more mole mayhem. It seems the merry-go-round isn't the only thing missing in action.

Farther down the hall, Logan stumbles upon something even more disturbing....

Before Logan can do anything rash, the school suddenly starts to shake and

Logan and Gustavo run outside to find the playground swings swinging out of control and the seesaws teetering and tottering violently. Everything seems to be sinking into the earth!

Not one to stand by and watch all her fellow students get pulled under, Logan swings out onto the monkey bars to rescue little Charlie Richards!

Gustavo jumps onto one end of the seesaw to save Bobby Bing, but for some reason, Bobby goes sailing into the air without even saying good-bye.

Wait! Don't go. I'm trying to rescue you!

Then Logan fishes Holly Peterson out of the sandbox with a tetherball pole while Gustavo directs the rest of the kids down the slide to safety.

Please put on your life vests and slide in single-file fashion. Thank you for flying Murkee Elementary!

When the dust finally settles, all that's left of the playground is a giant hole.

While Principal Shrub is pelted with sand, Logan and Gustavo peer over into the dark, foreboding pit.

We're gonna follow this tunnel till it takes us right to the suspects. What do you say, hotshot? Now's your chance to prove you're a master detective.

Do we have to?

CHAPTER 4
BEG, BURROW, OR STEAL

Logan and Gustavo explore the creepy cave beneath the playground. It's dark, moist, and chilly, like a congested polar bear's nostril. And did I mention it's dark? I mean really dark.

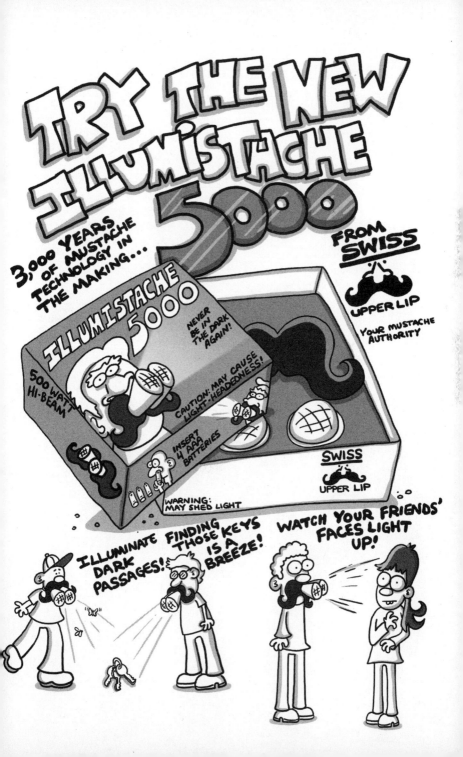

Gustavo's Illumistache quickly reveals a huge pile of boulders blocking their path.

62

A high-pitched, chipmunky voice blares out of a deranged mole's walkie-talkie....

If the students of Murkee Elementary want to see their merry-go-round, toys, and playground again, they will leave their lunch money on the second base of the softball field by 3:33 PM!

Perhaps if we could speak to you without your army of moles, we could negotiate....

If these critters want to negotiate, they'll have to do it with my foot! Prepare for combat!

64

The moles attack Gustavo with a Mighty Mach 5 Mega Maneuver, which he blocks with a Shaolin Super Shield!

Then they hit Logan with a Hyper Hedgehog High Kick, but she avoids it using her Timid Tenderfoot Technique!

It's the greatest martial arts fight scene ever! Unfortunately, since it's pitch-black, no one can see it. At least we saved some serious money on illustrations.

Logan and Gustavo finally crawl back out of
the hole, beaten and exhausted.

That blubbering glob of beef jerky is Ignas Scurge, the school bully....

CHAPTER 5

CURVEBALL

Murkee Elementary softball field, 3:30 PM. The lunch money is waiting on second base. Something else is waiting, too—ten hidden kids ready to pounce on whoever shows up to nab it.

DRINK

SNIG

TRY CHERRY, GRAPE, OR WILD ONION!

YOU CAN DO IT... PROBABLY!

Spot the hidden kids!

You two look pretty prepared.

Yep. We have a team of kids lying in wait, and we replaced second base with a replica made of solid concrete.

Yeah, if a mole digs up underneath this baby, he's gonna smack his noggin so hard, he'll need a hundred-pound Tylenol!

That's a pretty big Tylenol.

So, Logan and Gustavo wait...

and wait...

and wait...

It's 3:33 PM. I guess they're not coming.

Suddenly, a mole on a hang glider swoops in from above and swipes the bag of dough!

CHAPTER 6

HOMEWORK

When the last bell rings, Logan reluctantly lets Gustavo come over to work on the case.

If you're wondering why Logan's office is in an ice-cream truck, well, Logan's mom is an ice-cream man, uh, I mean *person*. She just got a fancy new truck with GPS and automatic fro-yo dispensers, so she's letting Logan use her old one to set up shop.

Gustavo is amazed by Logan's collection of mystery books...

her library of detective shows on video...

and her trophy from the Murkee City Break Dancing and Beat Box Championship?

Whoa! Look at those fly dance pants!

Give me those! I was, uh, in disguise on an important undercover operation.

Wheelie's 114 in dog years and has wheels on his hindquarters to help him get around. Most folks think he's always angry, but he actually has many moods:

Grumpy

Cranky

Furious

Cheesed off

Disappointed

About to bite you

Now that Gustavo and Wheelie are acquainted, Logan pulls out a marker and doodles on the world's biggest whiteboard.

She jots down everything that they know about
the suspect.

Gustavo offers his expertise as well....

Hey! Isn't he the guy who wrote the nerdy mole book you got from the library?

Logan whips out a map of the city to look for
Dr. Yonder's office at the Bureau of Burrowing.

CHAPTER 7
DEEPLY DISTURBING

Twenty minutes later, Logan and Gustavo roll up on their skateboards to the Bureau of Burrowing, in the heart of the Five Boroughs, in between Budrow's Burnished Bedroom Sets and Bureaus and Dos Burros Burritos. The joint is quiet. Too quiet. It's got Gustavo spooked.

Don't worry. Wheelie's here to protect us.

But who's gonna protect me from Wheelie?

Before entering the building, Logan reminds Gustavo and Wheelie that Dr. Yonder might help them solve the case, but he could also be the culprit. In fact…

everyone they talk to is a suspect! Remember that! The fate of humanity could depend on it!

Once they're inside, a hole in the floor opens, and a doctor bearing a big bowl of candy rises up. He offers the confections to Logan and Gustavo.

I suppose you're here about the curious criminal-mole incidents. It's certainly the most exciting development in burrowing mammals since the synchronized swimming shrews of Sri Lanka!

Don't mind if I do, Doc!

WHISTLER'S MOLE

Logan decides to put the pressure on Dr. Yonder....

91

Dr. Yonder gives the kids the grand tour of the underworld where he studies all things that live underground.

Dr. Yonder's lab is chock-full of beakers and gizmos and mole specimens. Across the room, Logan spots a strange device that resembles a bullhorn crossed with a fire extinguisher.

94

Dr. Yonder escorts them to his swanky office. Logan stops beating around the bush and asks him where he was yesterday at 4:25 PM, the time the merry-go-round went bye-bye.

Logan and Gustavo take off through Dr. Yonder's hall of prehistoric mole bones, with Wheelie burning rubber in the rear.

They reach the exit only to discover Dr. Yonder brandishing a long metal torture device!

Back at Logan's ice-cream truck headquarters, our two detectives discuss the case over a couple of cold Fudgysickles.

I hate to interrupt your all-you-can-eat Fudgysickle buffet, but Izzy Hurling is being interviewed on the local news!

CHAPTER 8
IZZY GUILTY?

Hurling Rivers Amusement Park. It's nearing closing time, and the park is as quiet as a mouse with a sock in its mouth. It's the perfect opportunity for Logan to get some answers.

They find Izzy in his office. He looks frantic and nervous as he flips through stacks of bills on his desk.

105

Izzy's violent allergic reaction to Wheelie leaves Logan and Gustavo with no choice but to leave his office empty-handed. They had thought this visit would bring answers, but instead, they leave with more questions and covered in old-man sneeze particles.

Wheelie takes it particularly hard. Just look at that sad face.

Our discouraged detectives slowly make their way out of the park and...Hey! Where are you two headed off to so fast?

Well, perhaps I should take this moment to remind you that the next lunch-money drop-off is

tomorrow at 5:27 PM!!!

No pressure. No pressure at all.

CHAPTER 9
DETENTION MOUNTS

The next morning at school, Principal Shrub is collecting lunch money from all the students, and, like a masseuse wearing boxing gloves, it rubs Logan the wrong way.

The sound of music suddenly catches their attention. It's the school bully, Ignas Scurge, and he's at his locker whistling a happy tune.

The sight of Ignas Scurge smiling and being nice sends Gustavo into a tizzy. Clearly, the case is breaking him.

It's all too much to handle! Missing merry-go-rounds, hang gliding moles, Ignas being nice! The world's gone nuts!

Don't let the pressure get to you, rookie. We just need to look at all the evidence one last time. The answer is there!

So, during lunch, instead of pouring gravy over Salisbury steak like the other students, Logan and Gustavo pore over the clues, notes, and doodles from the case....

Finally, Logan plants her finger on one of her doodles!

An Important Message from the Narrator

Hiya, punks! Since you wanna be detectives so bad, I thought I'd give you a chance to figure out whodunit before Logan and Gustavo spoil it in the next chapter. If you're stumped, go back and look at each page with a magnifying glass labeled "Suspect" or "Clue," like the ones right here.

Which one of these suspects is a low-down dirty crook?

 IZZY HURLING? He sure needed the money.

 DR. DEEP YONDER? He's a weirdo who knows his moles.

 IGNAS SCURGE? He loves stealing lunch money.

 PRINCIPAL SHRUB? He was all about paying off the thief.

Turn the page to find who dood it!

CHAPTER 10
A REVEALING ADDRESS

Hurling Rivers Amusement Park, 5:25 PM. Logan and Gustavo have three weeks' worth of lunch money waiting for the thief. But, to make things more interesting, they've also invited the entire student body of Murkee Elementary, the city police force, the media, and a dog on wheels.

Gustavo steps up to a podium in front of the spectators and law enforcement officials. He's wearing his Studly Stache LX to impress the crowd.

Ladies and gentlemen! One of you is a filthy, rotten criminal! The rest of you, I'm sure, are lovely people. We have called you here to reveal the identity of the scoundrel who has been training moles to steal the fun away from our city's youth.

WELCOME CITIZENS

NO FLASH PHOTOGRAPHY

JUSTICE

120

Logan turns her attention to the owner of Hurling Rivers....

Even the school principal isn't above suspicion.

The crowd roars with laughter. Principal Shrub doesn't take it too well.

With Shrub ruled out as the criminal, it leaves just one other suspect....

Uh, call me crazy, but I think you need proof
before you can just make accusations like that.

Suddenly, Ignas jumps up onto the podium like a frog with ants in his button-fly jeans and confesses to the whole kit and caboodle.

Captain Mosely steps up to make the arrest.

With a mighty tremor, the earth suddenly opens up like an overstuffed piñata. Hundreds of attack moles leap out and wreak havoc on the public. But that's just a warm-up....

Right behind the normal-size moles is one abnormal, gargantuan, *gigante*, behemoth-tastic robo-mole, built from the missing merry-go-round and scrap metal from the stolen playground!

The mecha-beast lays waste to the park!

The cries of stranded park riders grab Logan's attention, and she swings out like Tarzan to rescue a tot off the Junior Jungle Terror Cruise!

Wheelie rolls out onto the bumper-car course to save a terrified mother and her swaddled babe!

And Gustavo rescues the last funnel cake from a bubbling pit of hot grease!

Come to Papa!

Dr. Deep Yonder steps in to offer his expertise. If Logan and Gustavo can activate his Mole Disser 5000, tragedy can be averted.

Unfortunately, the device got lost in the stampede!
Whatever shall we do? Oh me, oh my!

Logan takes matters into her own hands. And when I say "matters," I mean Gustavo's 'stache.

With a mighty toss, Logan lets the facial hair fly!

The Mole Disser 5000 unleashes a stream of insults!

Even the metal monster collapses in a twisted heap! It must have been sensitive to insults as well.

But Captain Mosely has other ideas....

137

138

139

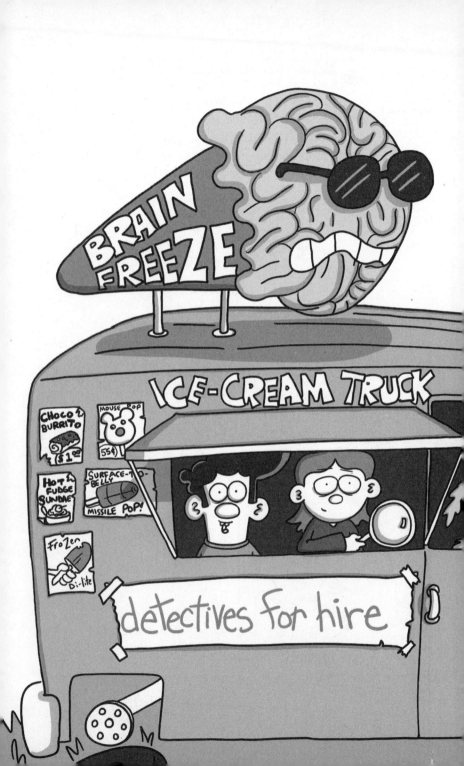

CHAPTER 11
MAKE THAT A DOUBLE SCOOP

1411 Baskerville Lane, 4:34 PM. A bold new detective duo sits in their refurbished office, ready for cases of mystery, intrigue, and mild excitement to come pouring in.

To make time for the new business, Gustavo has to give up his weekly Macho Cop Club for Kids meetings.

They come up with a clever name using the process of elimination—meaning Logan quickly eliminates all of Gustavo's suggestions.

They hire a friendly canine bodyguard.

And Logan hooks Gustavo up with his own desk, filled with six-month-old Fudgysickles.

Then they sit and wait...and wait...

and wait...and wait....

DOODLE SNOOPS

CLASSIFIED

Warning:
The following secret files may require doodling, scribbling, heavy thinking, and possible yodeling!

Hey! If you don't own this book, make sure you only doodle on a piece of scrap paper. If Miss Perusa finds any drawing on school property, she might staple your big toe to a math book!

MYSTERY
FICTION
HISTORY

LIBRARIAN

HOW TO DRAW LOGAN

1. Start with the eyes, like the lenses from a pair of sunglasses.

2. Just like school, they need pupils.

3. Add a cute little nose.

4. Then the face, like a soup bowl with ears.

5. Then some hair, like your mom's drapes.

6. Finish with some shoulders and a sly grin. There you have it!

Visit lb-kids.com to print out these activities.

HOW TO DRAW GUSTAVO

1. Start with two orbs, like two plump olives.

2. Draw a schnoz, like a fat jelly bean.

3. Add a head, like a large soda with ears.

4. Don't forget the stylish hair.

5. How about a manly mustache?

6. Hire your three-year-old brother to color It in and voilà!

HOW TO DRAW AN ANGRY MOLE

1. Draw a snout, like a balloon with two strings.

2. Add some angry eyes.

3. How about some jagged teeth?

4. And an arm with sharp claws, like a pointy garden tool.

5. Give it a terrible case of back hair.

6. And don't forget the pretty bow! Congrats! You're done!

Visit lb-kids.com to print out these activities.

1. Start with two mad eyeballs.

2. Add a snout, like an upside-down turnip.

3. Give him a shaggy mustache, like two bird wings.

4. Some snarly teeth and a beard.

5. Add floppy ears, like a bunny with a fur condition. And a long neck, too.

6. Be sure to add plenty of slobber for authenticity. Now, back off! He just might bite you!

WHAT'S UNDER LOGAN'S MAGNIFYING GLASS?

Sketch the magnified clue!

- It has six legs.
- It oozes slime.
- It has three eyes.
- It wears high-top sneakers.
- It sings karaoke!

What's in Wheelie's dog bowl and why does it smell like blue cheese?

Something's eating Miss Myrtle's potted plants up on the fifth floor! Help the Snoop Troop catch the culprit by sketching the suspect. Here's an eyewitness description:

- It's tall with four long, skinny legs.
- It has splotchy spots all over.
- It has a seven-foot-long neck!
- It has a tail with a tuft of hair on the end.
- It has big eyes with luscious lashes.
- It was last seen with a mouthful of chewed petunias.

Visit lb-kids.com to print out these activities.

Hide as many moles as you can in the theme park!

Make sure they're extra hidden! The Snoop Troop is here to sniff them out!

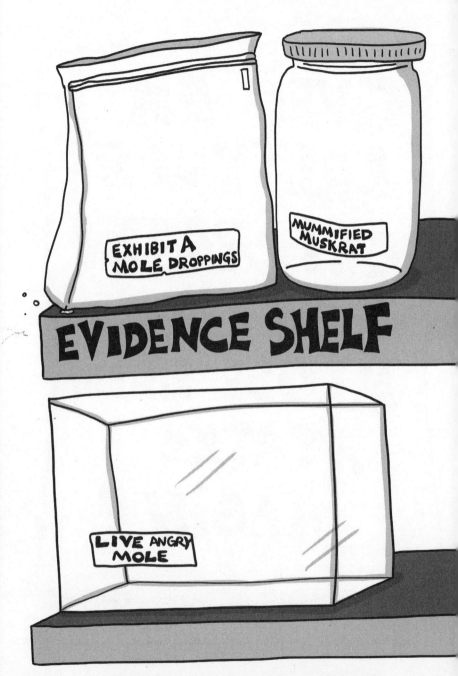

EXHIBIT A
MOLE DROPPINGS

MUMMIFIED
MUSKRAT

EVIDENCE SHELF

LIVE ANGRY
MOLE

Visit lb-kids.com to print out this activity.

Fill in all the gross details!

WORD SEARCH

A	B	M	B	L	N	X	Z	D	F	U	R	R	Y	A	C	D
Q	I	D	P	E	T	S	T	O	R	E	U	P	W	I	S	L
U	T	N	O	L	H	L	C	I	D	K	R	A	N	S	O	M
I	E	S	O	B	U	N	D	E	R	G	R	O	U	N	D	J
P	R	A	I	R	I	E	D	O	G	Y	F	K	D	B	Q	H
S	R	T	H	N	C	C	E	U	L	O	R	F	M	C	L	A
T	U	R	R	Y	L	L	A	B	O	R	A	T	O	R	Y	I
E	B	A	Q	D	U	Y	D	P	I	P	U	R	L	F	E	R
A	T	U	N	N	E	L	I	K	G	A	D	J	E	T	S	Y
L	B	Z	R	O	S	W	G	P	B	U	R	R	O	W	E	S

FIND THE WORDS INVOLVING CRIMINAL UNDERGROUND CRITTERS!

Answers on page 168!

Visit lb-kids.com to print out these activities.

163

Answers on page 168!

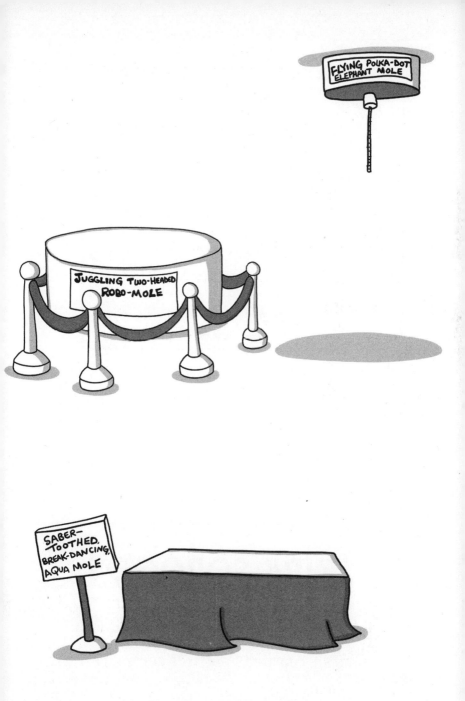

DOODLE SNOOPS ANSWER KEY

WORD SEARCH:

```
A  B  M  B  L  N  X  Z  D (F  U  R  R  Y) A  C  D
Q  I  D (P  E  T  S  T  O  R  E) U  P  W  I  S  L
U  T  N  O  L  H  L  C  I  D  K (R  A  N  S  O  M)
I  E  S  O  B (U  N  D  E  R  G  R  O  U  N  D) J
(P  R  A  I  R  I  E  D  O  G) Y  F  K  D  B  Q  H
S  R  T  H  N  C  C  E  U  L  O  R  F  M  C  L  A
T  U  R  R  Y  L (L  A  B  O  R  A  T  O  R  Y) I
E  B  A  Q  D  U  Y  D  P  I  P  U  R  L  F  E  R
A (T  U  N  N  E  L) I  K  G  A  D  J  E  T  S  Y
L  B  Z  R  O  S  W  G  P (B  U  R  R  O  W) E  S
```

MOLE DISSER 5000 PARTS:

1. Page 164: on the clown's hat
2. Page 164: in the man's hand
3. Page 165: on the counter by the condiments
4. Page 165: the lady's earring
5. Page 165: on the boy's head
6. Page 165: on the ground under the bench

KIRK SCROGGS

is the author and illustrator of the Tales of a Sixth-Grade Muppet series and the Wiley & Grampa's Creature Features series. He lives in Los Angeles.